'The youn
the sceni
glanced nervously
down the sofa at the
girl in the fringed
dress. She was
examining her hand-
kerchief; it might have
been the first one of
its kind she had seen,
so deep was her
interest in its material,
form, and possibilities'

DOROTHY PARKER

Born 22 August 1893, Long Branch, New Jersey
Died 7 June 1967, New York City, New York State

'The Sexes', 'The Lovely Leave', 'The Little Hours', 'Glory in the Daytime' and 'Lolita' first appeared in book form in *The Portable Dorothy Parker* in 1944.

ALSO PUBLISHED BY PENGUIN BOOKS

The Collected Dorothy Parker · *The Ladies of the Corridor*

DOROTHY PARKER

The Sexes

PENGUIN BOOKS

PENGUIN CLASSICS

Published by the Penguin Group
Penguin Books Ltd, 80 Strand, London WC2R 0RL, England
Penguin Group (USA), Inc., 375 Hudson Street, New York, New York 10014, USA
Penguin Group (Canada), 90 Eglinton Avenue East, Suite 700, Toronto, Ontario, Canada M4P 2Y3 (a division of Pearson Penguin Canada Inc.)
Penguin Ireland, 25 St Stephen's Green, Dublin 2, Ireland (a division of Penguin Books Ltd)
Penguin Group (Australia), 250 Camberwell Road, Camberwell, Victoria 3124, Australia (a division of Pearson Australia Group Pty Ltd)
Penguin Books India Pvt Ltd, 11 Community Centre, Panchsheel Park, New Delhi – 110 017, India
Penguin Group (NZ), 67 Apollo Drive, Rosedale, North Shore 0632, New Zealand (a division of Pearson New Zealand Ltd)
Penguin Books (South Africa) (Pty) Ltd, 24 Sturdee Avenue, Rosebank, Johannesburg 2196, South Africa

Penguin Books Ltd, Registered Offices: 80 Strand, London WC2R 0RL, England

www.penguin.com

Selected from *The Collected Dorothy Parker*, published in Penguin Classics 2001
This edition published in Penguin Classics 2011
1

Typeset by Jouve (UK), Milton Keynes
Printed in England by Clays Ltd, St Ives plc

ISBN: 978-0-141-19619-0

www.greenpenguin.co.uk

Contents

The Sexes

The young man with the scenic cravat glanced nervously down the sofa at the girl in the fringed dress. She was examining her handkerchief; it might have been the first one of its kind she had seen, so deep was her interest in its material, form, and possibilities. The young man cleared his throat, without necessity or success, producing a small, syncopated noise.

'Want a cigarette?' he said.

'No, thank you,' she said. 'Thank you ever so much just the same.'

'Sorry I've only got these kind,' he said. 'You got any of your own?'

'I really don't know,' she said. 'I probably have, thank you.'

'Because if you haven't,' he said, 'it wouldn't take me a minute to go up to the corner and get you some.'

'Oh, thank you, but I wouldn't have you go to all that

trouble for anything,' she said. 'It's awfully sweet of you to think of it. Thank you ever so much.'

'Will you for God's sakes stop thanking me?' he said.

'Really,' she said, 'I didn't know I was saying anything out of the way. I'm awfully sorry if I hurt your feelings. I know what it feels like to get your feelings hurt. I'm sure I didn't realize it was an insult to say "thank you" to a person. I'm not exactly in the habit of having people swear at me because I say "thank you" to them.'

'I did not swear at you!' he said.

'Oh, you didn't?' she said. 'I see.'

'My God,' he said, 'all I said, I simply asked you if I couldn't go out and get you some cigarettes. Is there anything in that to get up in the air about?'

'Who's up in the air?' she said. 'I'm sure I didn't know it was a criminal offense to say I wouldn't dream of giving you all that trouble. I'm afraid I must be awfully stupid, or something.'

'Do you want me to go out and get you some cigarettes; or don't you?' he said.

'Goodness,' she said, 'if you want to go so much, please don't feel you have to stay here. I wouldn't have you feel you had to stay for anything.'

'Ah, don't be that way, will you?' he said.

'Be what way?' she said. 'I'm not being any way.'

'What's the matter?' he said.

'Why, nothing,' she said. 'Why?'

'You've been funny all evening,' he said. 'Hardly said a word to me, ever since I came in.'

'I'm terribly sorry you haven't been having a good time,' she said. 'For goodness' sakes, don't feel you have to stay here and be bored. I'm sure there are millions of places you could be having a lot more fun. The only thing, I'm a little bit sorry I didn't know before, that's all. When you said you were coming over tonight, I broke a lot of dates to go to the theater and everything. But it doesn't make a bit of difference. I'd much rather have you go and have a good time. It isn't very pleasant to sit here and feel you're boring a person to death.'

'I'm not bored!' he said. 'I don't want to go any place! Ah, honey, won't you tell me what's the matter? Ah, please.'

'I haven't the faintest idea what you're talking about,' she said. 'There isn't a thing on earth the matter. I don't know what you mean.'

'Yes, you do,' he said. 'There's something the trouble. Is it anything I've done, or anything?'

'Goodness,' she said, 'I'm sure it isn't any of my business, anything you do. I certainly wouldn't feel I had any right to criticize.'

'Will you stop talking like that?' he said. 'Will you, please?'

'Talking like what?' she said.

'You know,' he said. 'That's the way you were talking over the telephone today, too. You were so snotty when I called you up, I was afraid to talk to you.'

'I beg your pardon,' she said. 'What did you say I was?'

'Well, I'm sorry,' he said. 'I didn't mean to say that. You get me so balled up.'

'You see,' she said, 'I'm really not in the habit of hearing language like that. I've never had a thing like that said to me in my life.'

'I told you I was sorry, didn't I?' he said. 'Honest, honey, I didn't mean it. I don't know how I came to say a thing like that. Will you excuse me? Please?'

'Oh, certainly,' she said. 'Goodness, don't feel you have to apologize to me. It doesn't make any difference at all. It just seems a little bit funny to have somebody you were in the habit of thinking was a gentleman come to your home and use language like that to you, that's all. But it doesn't make the slightest bit of difference.'

'I guess nothing I say makes any difference to you,' he said. 'You seem to be sore at me.'

'I'm sore at you?' she said. 'I can't understand what

put that idea in your head. Why should I be sore at you?'

'That's what I'm asking you,' he said. 'Won't you tell me what I've done? Have I done something to hurt your feelings, honey? The way you were, over the phone, you had me worried all day. I couldn't do a lick of work.'

'I certainly wouldn't like to feel,' she said, 'that I was interfering with your work. I know there are lots of girls that don't think anything of doing things like that, but I think it's terrible. It certainly isn't very nice to sit here and have someone tell you you interfere with his business.'

'I didn't say that!' he said. 'I didn't say it!'

'Oh, didn't you?' she said. 'Well, that was the impression I got. It must be my stupidity.'

'I guess maybe I better go,' he said. 'I can't get right. Everything I say seems to make you sorer and sorer. Would you rather I'd go?'

'Please do just exactly whatever you like,' she said. 'I'm sure the last thing I want to do is have you stay here when you'd rather be some place else. Why don't you go some place where you won't be bored? Why don't you go up to Florence Leaming's? I know she'd love to have you.'

'I don't want to go up to Florence Leaming's!' he

said. 'What would I want to go up to Florence Leaming's for? She gives me a pain.'

'Oh, really?' she said. 'She didn't seem to be giving you so much of a pain at Elsie's party last night, I notice. I notice you couldn't even talk to anybody else, that's how much of a pain she gave you.'

'Yeah, and you know why I was talking to her?' he said.

'Why, I suppose you think she's attractive,' she said. 'I suppose some people do. It's perfectly natural. Some people think she's quite pretty.'

'I don't know whether she's pretty or not,' he said. 'I wouldn't know her if I saw her again. Why I was talking to her was you wouldn't even give me a tumble, last night. I came up and tried to talk to you, and you just said, "Oh, how do you do" – just like that, "Oh, how do you do" – and you turned right away and wouldn't look at me.'

'I wouldn't look at you?' she said. 'Oh, that's awfully funny. Oh, that's marvelous. You don't mind if I laugh, do you?'

'Go ahead and laugh your head off,' he said. 'But you wouldn't.'

'Well, the minute you came in the room,' she said, 'you started making such a fuss over Florence Leaming, I thought you never wanted to see anybody else. You two seemed to be having such a wonderful time together, goodness knows I wouldn't have butted in for anything.'

'My God,' he said, 'this what's-her-name girl came up and began talking to me before I even saw anybody else, and what could I do? I couldn't sock her in the nose, could I?'

'I certainly didn't see you try,' she said.

'You saw me try to talk to you, didn't you?' he said. 'And what did you do? "Oh, how do you do." Then this what's-her-name came up again, and there I was, stuck. Florence Leaming! I think she's terrible. Know what I think of her? I think she's a damn little fool. That's what I think of her.'

'Well, of course,' she said, 'that's the impression she always gave me, but I don't know. I've heard people say she's pretty. Honestly I have.'

'Why, she can't be pretty in the same room with you,' he said.

'She has got an awfully funny nose,' she said. 'I really feel sorry for a girl with a nose like that.'

'She's got a terrible nose,' he said. 'You've got a beautiful nose. Gee, you've got a pretty nose.'

'Oh, I have not,' she said. 'You're crazy.'

'And beautiful eyes,' he said, 'and beautiful hair and a beautiful mouth. And beautiful hands. Let me have one of the little hands. Ah, look atta little hand! Who's got the prettiest hands in the world? Who's the sweetest girl in the world?'

'I don't know,' she said. 'Who?'

'You don't know!' he said. 'You do so, too, know.'

'I do not,' she said. 'Who? Florence Leaming?'

'Oh, Florence Leaming, my eye!' he said. 'Getting sore about Florence Leaming! And me not sleeping all last night and not doing a stroke of work all day because you wouldn't speak to me! A girl like you getting sore about a girl like Florence Leaming!'

'I think you're just perfectly crazy,' she said. 'I was not sore! What on earth ever made you think I was? You're simply crazy. Ow, my new pearl beads! Wait a second till I take them off. There!'

The Lovely Leave

Her husband had telephoned her by long distance to tell her about the leave. She had not expected the call, and she had no words arranged. She threw away whole seconds explaining her surprise at hearing him, and reporting that it was raining hard in New York, and asking was it terribly hot where he was. He had stopped her to say, look, he didn't have time to talk long; and he had told her quickly that his squadron was to be moved to another field the next week and on the way he would have twenty-four hours' leave. It was difficult for her to hear. Behind his voice came a jagged chorus of young male voices, all crying the syllable 'Hey!'

'Ah, don't hang up yet,' she said. 'Please. Let's talk another minute, just another – '

'Honey, I've got to go,' he said. 'The boys all want a crack at the telephone. See you a week from today, around five. 'By.'

Then there had been a click as his receiver went back

into place. Slowly she cradled her telephone, looking at it as if all frustrations and bewilderments and separations were its fault. Over it she had heard his voice, coming from far away. All the months, she had tried not to think of the great blank distance between them; and now that far voice made her know she had thought of nothing else. And his speech had been brisk and busy. And from back of him had come gay, wild young voices, voices he heard every day and she did not, voices of those who shared his new life. And he had heeded them and not her, when she begged for another minute. She took her hand off the telephone and held it away from her with the fingers spread stiffly apart, as if it had touched something horrid.

Then she told herself to stop her nonsense. If you looked for things to make you feel hurt and wretched and unnecessary, you were certain to find them, more easily each time, so easily, soon, that you did not even realize you had gone out searching. Women alone often developed into experts at the practice. She must never join their dismal league.

What was she dreary about, anyway? If he had only a little while to talk, then he had only a little while to talk, that was all. Certainly he had had time to tell her he was coming, to say that they would be together soon. And there she was, sitting scowling at the telephone, the kind, faithful telephone that had brought her the lovely news. She would see him in a week. Only a week. She began to feel, along her back and through her middle, little quivers of excitement, like tiny springs uncoiling into spirals.

There must be no waste to this leave. She thought of the preposterous shyness that had fallen upon her when he had come home before. It was the first time she had seen him in uniform. There he stood, in their little apartment, a dashing stranger in strange, dashing garments. Until he had gone into the army, they had never spent a night apart in all their marriage; and when she saw him, she dropped her eyes and twisted her handkerchief and could bring nothing but monosyllables from her throat. There must be no such squandering of minutes this time. There must be no such gangling diffidence to lop even an instant from their twenty-four hours of perfect union. Oh, Lord, only twenty-four hours . . .

No. That was exactly the wrong thing to do; that was directly the wrong way to think. That was the way she had spoiled it before. Almost as soon as the shyness had left her and she felt she knew him again, she had begun counting. She was so filled with the desperate consciousness of the hours sliding away – only twelve more, only five, oh, dear God, only one left – that she had no room for gaiety and ease. She had spent the golden time in grudging its going.

She had been so woebegone of carriage, so sad and slow of word as the last hour went, that he, nervous under the pall, had spoken sharply and there had been a quarrel. When he had had to leave for his train, there were no clinging farewells, no tender words to keep. He had gone to the door and opened it and stood with it against his shoulder while he shook out his flight cap and put it on, adjusting it with great care, one inch over the eye, one inch above the ear. She stood in the middle of the living-room, cool and silent, looking at him.

When his cap was precisely as it should be, he looked at her.

'Well,' he said. He cleared his throat. 'Guess I'd better get going.'

'I'm sure you had,' she said.

He studied his watch intently. 'I'll just make it,' he said.

'I'm sure you will,' she said.

She turned, not with an actual shrug, only with the effect of one, and went to the window and looked out, as if casually remarking the weather. She heard the door close loudly and then the grind of the elevator.

When she knew he was gone, she was cool and still no longer. She ran about the little flat, striking her breast and sobbing.

Then she had two months to ponder what had

happened, to see how she had wrought the ugly small ruin. She cried in the nights.

She need not brood over it any more. She had her lesson; she could forget how she had learned it. This new leave would be the one to remember, the one he and she would have, to keep forever. She was to have a second chance, another twenty-four hours with him. After all, that is no short while, you know; that is, if you do not think of it as a thin little row of hours dropping off like beads from a broken string. Think of it as a whole long day and a whole long night, shining and sweet, and you will be all but awed by your fortune. For how many people are there who have the memory of a whole long day and a whole long night, shining and sweet, to carry with them in their hearts until they die?

To keep something, you must take care of it. More, you must understand just what sort of care it requires. You must know the rules and abide by them. She could do that. She had been doing it all the months, in the writing of her letters to him. There had been rules to be learned in that matter, and the first of them was the hardest: never say to him what you want him to say to you. Never tell him how sadly you miss him, how it grows no better, how each day without him is sharper than the day before. Set down for him the gay happenings about you, bright little anecdotes, not invented, necessarily, but attractively embellished. Do not bedevil him with the pinings of your faithful heart because he is your husband, your man, your love. For you are writing to none of these. You are writing to a soldier.

She knew those rules. She would have said that she would rather die, and she would have meant something very near the words, than send a letter of complaint or sadness or cold anger to her husband, a soldier far away, strained and weary from his work, giving all he had for the mighty cause. If in her letters she could be all he wanted her to be, how much easier to be it when they were together. Letters were difficult; every word had to be considered and chosen. When they were together again, when they could see and hear and touch each other, there would be no stiltedness. They would talk and laugh together. They would have tenderness and excitement. It would be as if they had never been separated. Perhaps they never had been. Perhaps a strange new life and strange empty miles and strange gay voices had no existence for two who were really one.

She had thought it out. She had learned the laws of what not to do. Now she could give herself up to the ecstasy of waiting his coming.

It was a fine week. She counted the time again, but now it was sweet to see it go. Two days after tomorrow, day after tomorrow, tomorrow. She lay awake in the dark, but it was a thrilling wakefulness. She went tall and straight by day, in pride in her warrior. On the street, she looked with amused pity at women who walked with men in civilian suits.

She bought a new dress; black – he liked black dresses – simple – he liked plain dresses – and so expensive that she would not think of its price. She charged it, and realized that for months to come she would tear up the bill without removing it from its envelope. All right – this was no time to think of months to come.

The day of the leave was a Saturday. She flushed with gratitude to the army for this coincidence, for after one o'clock, Saturday was her own. She went from her office without stopping for lunch, and bought perfume and toilet water and bath oil. She had a bit of each remaining in bottles on her dressing table and in her bathroom, but it made her feel desired and secure to have rich new stores of them. She bought a nightgown, a delightful thing of soft chiffon patterned with little bouquets, with innocent puffs of sleeves and a Romney neck and a blue sash. It could never withstand laundering, a French cleaner must care for it – all right. She hurried home with it, to fold it in a satin sachet.

Then she went out again and bought the materials for cocktails and whiskies-and-sodas, shuddering at their cost. She went a dozen blocks to buy the kind of salted biscuits he liked with drinks. On the way back she passed a florist's shop in the window of which were displayed potted fuchsia. She made no attempt to resist them. They were too charming, with their delicate parchment-colored inverted cups and their graceful magenta bells. She bought six pots of them. Suppose she did without lunches the next week – all right.

When she was done with the little living-room, it looked gracious and gay. She ranged the pots of fuchsia along the window sill, she drew out a table and set it with glasses and bottles, she plumped the pillows and laid bright-covered magazines about invitingly. It was a place where someone entering eagerly would find delighted welcome.

Before she changed her dress, she telephoned downstairs to the man who tended both the switchboard and the elevator.

'Oh,' she said, when he eventually answered. 'Oh, I just want to say, when my husband, Lieutenant McVicker, comes, please send him right up.'

There was no necessity for the call. The wearied attendant would have brought up anyone to any flat without the additional stress of a telephoned announcement. But she wanted to say the words. She wanted to say 'my husband' and she wanted to say 'lieutenant'.

She sang, when she went into the bedroom to dress.

She had a sweet, uncertain little voice that made the lusty song ludicrous.

> *'Off we go, into the wild blue yonder.*
> *Climbing high into the sun, sun, sun, sun.*
> *Here they come; zooming to meet our thunder –*
> *At 'em boys, give 'er the gun!'*

She kept singing, in a preoccupied way, while she gave close attention to her lips and her eyelashes. Then she was silent and held her breath as she drew on the new dress. It was good to her. There was a reason for the cost of those perfectly plain black dresses. She stood looking at herself in the mirror with deep interest, as if she watched a chic unknown, the details of whose costume she sought to memorize.

As she stood there, the bell rang. It rang three times, loud and quick. He had come.

She gasped, and her hands fluttered over the dressing table. She seized the perfume atomizer and sprayed scent violently all about her head and shoulders, some of it reaching them. She had already perfumed herself, but she wanted another minute, another moment, anything. For it had taken her again – the outrageous shyness. She could not bring herself to go to the door and open it. She stood, shaking, and squirted perfume.

The bell rang three times loud and quick again, and then an endless peal.

'Oh, *wait*, can't you?' she cried. She threw down the atomizer, looked wildly around the room as if for a hiding-place, then sternly made herself tall and sought to control the shaking of her body. The shrill noise of the bell seemed to fill the flat and crowd the air out of it.

She started for the door. Before she reached it, she stopped, held her hands over her face, and prayed, 'Oh, please let it be all right,' she whispered. 'Please keep me from doing wrong things. Please let it be lovely.'

Then she opened the door. The noise of the bell stopped. There he stood in the brightly lighted little hall. All the long sad nights, and all the strong and sensible vows. And now he had come. And there she stood.

'Well, for heaven's sake!' she said. 'I had no idea there was anybody out here. Why, you were just as quiet as a little mouse.'

'Well! Don't you ever open the door?' he said.

'Can't a woman have time to put on her shoes?' she said.

He came in and closed the door behind him. 'Ah, darling,' he said. He put his arms around her. She slid her cheek along his lips, touched her forehead to his shoulder, and broke away from him.

'Well!' she said. 'Nice to see you, Lieutenant. How's the war?'

'How are you?' he said. 'You look wonderful.'

'Me?' she said. 'Look at you.'

He was well worth looking at. His fine clothes complemented his fine body. The precision of his appointments was absolute, yet he seemed to have no consciousness of it. He stood straight, and he moved with grace and assurance. His face was browned. It was thin, so thin that the bones showed under the cheeks and down the jaws; but there was no look of strain in it. It was smooth and serene and confident. He was the American officer, and there was no finer sight than he.

'Well!' she said. She made herself raise her eyes to his and found suddenly that it was no longer difficult. 'Well, we can't just stand here saying "well" at each other. Come on in and sit down. We've got a long time ahead of us – oh, Steve, isn't it wonderful! Hey. Didn't you bring a bag?'

'Why, you see,' he said, and stopped. He slung his cap over onto the table among the bottles and glasses. 'I left the bag at the station. I'm afraid I've got sort of rotten news, darling.'

She kept her hands from flying to her breast.

'You – you're going overseas right away?' she said.

'Oh, Lord, no,' he said. 'Oh, no, no, no. I said this

was rotten news. No. They've changed the orders, baby. They've taken back all leaves. We're to go right on to the new field. I've got to get a train at six-ten.'

She sat down on the sofa. She wanted to cry; not silently with slow crystal tears, but with wide mouth and smeared face. She wanted to throw herself stomach-down on the floor, and kick and scream, and go limp if anyone tried to lift her.

'I think that's awful,' she said. 'I think that's just filthy.'

'I know,' he said. 'But there's nothing to do about it. This is the army, Mrs Jones.'

'Couldn't you have said something?' she said. 'Couldn't you have told them you've had only one leave in six months? Couldn't you have said all the chance your wife had to see you again was just this poor little twenty-four hours? Couldn't you have explained what it meant to her? Couldn't you?'

'Come on, now, Mimi,' he said. 'There's a war on.'

'I'm sorry,' she said. 'I was sorry as soon as I'd said it. I was sorry while I was saying it. But – oh, it's so hard!'

'It's not easy for anybody,' he said. 'You don't know how the boys were looking forward to their leaves.'

'Oh, I don't give a damn about the boys!' she said.

'That's the spirit that'll win for our side,' he said. He

sat down in the biggest chair, stretched his legs and crossed his ankles.

'You don't care about anything but those pilots,' she said.

'Look, Mimi,' he said. 'We haven't got time to do this. We haven't got time to get into a fight and say a lot of things we don't mean. Everything's all – all speeded up, now. There's no time left for this.'

'Oh, I know,' she said. 'Oh, Steve, don't I know!'

She went over and sat on the arm of his chair and buried her face in his shoulder.

'This is more like it,' he said. 'I've kept thinking about this.' She nodded against his blouse.

'If you knew what it was to sit in a decent chair again,' he said.

She sat up 'Oh,' she said. 'It's the chair. I'm so glad you like it.'

'They've got the worst chairs you ever saw, in the pilots' room,' he said. 'A lot of busted-down old rockers – honestly, rockers – that big-hearted patriots contributed, to get them out of the attic. If they haven't better furniture at the new field. I'm going to do something about it, even if I have to buy the stuff myself.'

'I certainly would, if I were you,' she said. 'I'd go without food and clothing and laundry, so the boys would be happy sitting down. I wouldn't even save out enough for air mail stamps, to write to my wife once in a while.'

She rose and moved about the room.

'Mimi, what's the matter with you?' he said. 'Are you – are you jealous of the pilots?'

She counted as far as eight, to herself. Then she turned and smiled at him.

'Why – I guess I am – ' she said. 'I guess that's just what I must be. Not only of the pilots. Of the whole air corps. Of the whole Army of the United States.'

'You're wonderful,' he said.

'You see,' she said with care, 'you have a whole new life – I have half an old one. Your life is so far away from mine, I don't see how they're ever going to come back together.'

'That's nonsense,' he said.

'No, please wait,' she said. 'I get strained and – and frightened, I guess, and I say things I could cut my throat for saying. But you know what I really feel about you. I'm so proud of you I can't find words for it. I know you're doing the most important thing in the world, maybe the only important thing in the world. Only – oh, Steve, I wish to heaven you didn't love doing it so much!'

'Listen,' he said.

'No,' she said. 'You mustn't interrupt a lady. It's unbecoming an officer, like carrying packages in the street. I'm just trying to tell you a little about how I feel. I can't get used to being so completely left out. You don't wonder what I do, you don't want to find out what's in my head – why, you never even ask me how I am!'

'I do so!' he said. 'I asked you how you were the minute I came in.'

'That was white of you,' she said.

'Oh, for heaven's sake!' he said. 'I didn't have to ask you. I could see how you look. You look wonderful. I told you that.'

She smiled at him. 'Yes, you did, didn't you?' she said. 'And you sounded as if you meant it. Do you really like my dress?'

'Oh, yes,' he said. 'I always liked that dress on you.'

It was as if she turned to wood. 'This dress,' she said, enunciating with insulting distinctness, 'is brand new. I have never had it on before in my life. In case you are interested, I bought it especially for this occasion.'

'I'm sorry, honey,' he said. 'Oh, sure, now I see it's not the other one at all. I think it's great. I like you in black.'

'At moments like this,' she said, 'I almost wish I were in it for another reason.'

'Stop it,' he said. 'Sit down and tell me about yourself. What have you been doing?'

'Oh, nothing,' she said.

'How's the office?' he said.

'Dull,' she said. 'Dull as mud.'

'Who have you seen?' he said.

'Oh, nobody,' she said.

'Well, what do you *do?*' he said.

'In the evenings?' she said. 'Oh, I sit here and knit and read detective stories that it turns out I've read before.'

'I think that's all wrong of you,' he said. 'I think it's asinine to sit here alone, moping. That doesn't do any good to anybody. Why don't you go out more?'

'I hate to go out with just women,' she said.

'Well, why do you have to?' he said. 'Ralph's in town, isn't he? And John and Bill and Gerald. Why don't you go out with them? You're silly not to.'

'It hadn't occurred to me,' she said, 'that it was silly to keep faithful to one's husband.'

'Isn't that taking rather a jump?' he said. 'It's possible to go to dinner with a man and stay this side of adultery. And don't use words like "one's". You're awful when you're elegant.'

'I know,' she said. 'I never have any luck when I try. No. You're the one that's awful, Steve. You really are. I'm trying to show you a glimpse of my heart, to tell you how it feels when you're gone, how I don't want to be with anyone if I can't be with you. And all you say is,

I'm not doing any good to anybody. That'll be nice to think of when you go. You don't know what it's like for me here alone. You just don't know.'

'Yes, I do,' he said. 'I know, Mimi.' He reached for a cigarette on the little table beside him, and the bright magazine by the cigarette-box caught his eye. 'Hey, is this this week's? I haven't seen it yet.' He glanced through the early pages.

'Go ahead and read if you want to,' she said. 'Don't let me disturb you.'

'I'm not reading,' he said. He put down the magazine. 'You see, I don't know what to say, when you start talking about showing me glimpses of your heart, and all that. I know. I know you must be having a rotten time. But aren't you feeling fairly sorry for yourself?'

'If *I'm* not,' she said, 'who would be?'

'What do you want anyone to be sorry for you for?' he said. 'You'd be all right if you'd stop sitting around alone. I'd like to think of you having a good time while I'm away.'

She went over to him and kissed him on the forehead.

'Lieutenant,' she said, 'you are a far nobler character than I am. Either that,' she said, 'or there is something else back of this.'

'Oh, shut up,' he said. He pulled her down to him

and held her there. She seemed to melt against him, and stayed there, still.

Then she felt him take his left arm from around her and felt his head raised from its place against hers. She looked up at him. He was craning over her shoulder, endeavoring to see his wristwatch.

'Oh, now, really!' she said. She put her hands against his chest and pushed herself vigorously away from him.

'It goes so quickly,' he said softly, with his eyes on his watch. 'We've – we've only a little while, darling.'

She melted again. 'Oh, Steve,' she whispered. 'Oh, dearest.'

'I do want to take a bath,' he said. 'Get up, will you, baby?'

She got right up. 'You're going to take a bath?' she said

'Yes,' he said. 'You don't mind, do you?'

'Oh, not in the least,' she said. 'I'm sure you'll enjoy it. It's one of the pleasantest ways of killing time, I always think.'

'You know how you feel after a long ride on a train,' he said.

'Oh, surely,' she said.

He rose and went into the bedroom. 'I'll hurry up,' he called back to her.

'Why?' she said.

Then she had a moment to consider herself. She went into the bedroom after him, sweet with renewed resolve. He had hung his blouse and necktie neatly over a chair and he was unbuttoning his shirt. As she came in, he took it off. She looked at the beautiful brown triangle of his back. She would do anything for him, anything in the world.

'I – I'll go run your bath water,' she said. She went into the bathroom, turned on the faucets of the tub, and set the towels and mat ready. When she came back into the bedroom he was just entering it from the living-room, naked. In his hand he carried the bright magazine he had glanced at before. She stopped short.

'Oh,' she said. 'You're planning to read in the tub?'

'If you knew how I'd been looking forward to this!' he said. 'Boy, a hot bath in a tub! We haven't got anything but showers, and when you take a shower, there's a hundred boys waiting, yelling at you to hurry up and get out.'

'I suppose they can't bear being parted from you,' she said.

He smiled at her. 'See you in a couple of minutes,' he said, and went on into the bathroom and closed the door. She heard the slow slip and slide of water as he laid himself in the tub.

She stood just as she was. The room was lively with the perfume she had sprayed, too present, too insistent. Her eyes went to the bureau drawer where lay, wrapped in soft fragrance, the nightgown with the little bouquets and the Romney neck. She went over to the bathroom door, drew back her right foot, and kicked the base of the door so savagely that the whole frame shook.

'What, dear?' he called. 'Want something?'

'Oh, nothing,' she said. 'Nothing whatever. I've got everything any woman could possibly want, haven't I?'

'What?' he called. 'I can't hear you, honey.'

'Nothing,' she screamed.

She went into the living-room. She stood, breathing heavily, her fingernails scarring her palms, as she looked at the fuchsia blossoms, with their dirty parchment-colored cups, their vulgar magenta bells.

Her breath was quiet and her hands relaxed when he came into the living-room again. He had on his trousers and shirt, and his necktie was admirably knotted. He carried his belt. She turned to him. There were things she had meant to say, but she could do nothing but smile at him, when she saw him. Her heart turned liquid in her breast.

His brow was puckered. 'Look, darling,' he said. 'Have you got any brass polish?'

'Why, no,' she said. 'We haven't even got any brass.'

'Well, have you any nail polish – the colorless kind? A lot of the boys use that.'

'I'm sure it must look adorable on them,' she said. 'No, I haven't anything but rose-colored polish. Would that be of any use to you, heaven forbid?'

'No,' he said, and he seemed worried. 'Red wouldn't be any good at all. Hell, I don't suppose you've got a Blitz Cloth, have you? Or a Shine-O?'

'If I had the faintest idea what you were talking about,' she said, 'I might be better company for you.'

He held the belt out toward her. 'I want to shine my buckle,' he said.

'Oh . . . my . . . dear . . . sweet . . . gentle . . . Lord,' she said. 'We've got about ten minutes left, and you want to shine your belt buckle.'

'I don't like to report to a new C.O. with a dull belt buckle,' he said.

'It was bright enough for you to report to your wife in, wasn't it?' she said.

'Oh, stop that,' he said. 'You just won't understand, that's all.'

'It isn't that I won't understand,' she said. 'It's that I can't remember. I haven't been with a Boy Scout for so long.'

He looked at her. 'You're being great, aren't you?' he said. He looked around the room. 'There must be a cloth around somewhere – oh, this will do.' He caught up a pretty little cocktail napkin from the table of untouched bottles and glasses, sat down with his belt laid over his knees, and rubbed at the buckle.

She watched him for a moment, then rushed over to him and grasped his arm.

'Please,' she said. 'Please, I didn't mean it, Steve.'

'Please let me do this, will you?' he said. He wrenched his arm from her hand and went on with his polishing.

'You tell me I won't understand!' she cried. 'You won't understand anything about anybody else. Except those crazy pilots.'

'They're all right!' he said. 'They're fine kids. They're going to make great fighters.' He went on rubbing at his buckle.

'Oh, I know it!' she said. 'You know I know it. I don't mean it when I say things against them. How would I dare to mean it? They're risking their lives and their sight and their sanity, they're giving everything for – '

'Don't do that kind of talk, will you?' he said. He rubbed the buckle.

'I'm not doing any kind of talk!' she said. 'I'm trying to tell you something. Just because you've got on that pretty suit, you think you should never hear anything serious, never anything sad or wretched or disagreeable. You make me sick, that's what you do! I know, I know – I'm not trying to take anything away from you, I realize what you're doing, I told you what I think of it. Don't, for heaven's sake, think I'm mean enough to grudge you any happiness and excitement you can get out of it. I know it's hard for you. But it's never lonely, that's all I mean. You have companionships no – no wife can ever give you. I suppose it's the sense of hurry, maybe, the consciousness of living on borrowed time, the – the knowledge of what you're all going into together that makes the comradeship of men in war so firm, so fast. But won't you please try to understand how I feel? Won't you understand that it comes out of bewilderment and disruption and – and being frightened, I guess? Won't you understand what makes me do what I do, when I hate myself while I'm doing it? Won't you please understand? Darling, won't you please?'

He laid down the little napkin. 'I can't go through this kind of thing, Mimi,' he said. 'Neither can you.' He looked at his watch. 'Hey, it's time for me to go.'

She stood tall and stiff. 'I'm sure it is,' she said.

'I'd better put on my blouse,' he said.

'You might as well,' she said.

He rose, wove his belt through the loops of his trousers, and went into the bedroom. She went over to the window and stood looking out, as if casually remarking the weather.

She heard him come back into the room, but she did not turn around. She heard his steps stop, knew he was standing there.

'Mimi,' he said.

She turned toward him, her shoulders back, her chin high, cool, regal. Then she saw his eyes. They were no longer bright and gay and confident. Their blue was misty and they looked troubled; they looked at her as if they pleaded with her.

'Look, Mimi,' he said, 'do you think I want to do this? Do you think I want to be away from you? Do you think that this is what I thought I'd be doing now? In the years – well, in the years when we ought to be together.'

He stopped. Then he spoke again, but with difficulty. 'I can't talk about it. I can't even think about it – because if I did I couldn't do my job. But just because I don't talk about it doesn't mean I want to be doing what I'm doing. I want to be with you, Mimi. That's where I belong. You know that, darling. Don't you?'

He held his arms open to her. She ran to them. This time, she did not slide her cheek along his lips.

When he had gone, she stood a moment by the fuchsia plants, touching delicately, tenderly, the enchanting parchment-colored caps, the exquisite magenta bells.

The telephone rang. She answered it, to hear a friend

of hers inquiring about Steve, asking how he looked and how he was, urging that he come to the telephone and say hello to her.

'He's gone,' she said. 'All their leaves were canceled. He wasn't here an hour.'

The friend cried sympathy. It was a shame, it was simply awful, it was absolutely terrible.

'No, don't say that,' she said. 'I know it wasn't very much time. But oh, it was lovely!'

The Little Hours

Now what's this? What's the object of all this darkness all over me? They haven't gone and buried me alive while my back was turned, have they? Ah, now would you think they'd do a thing like that! Oh, no, I know what it is. I'm awake. That's it. I've waked up in the middle of the night. Well, isn't that nice. Isn't that simply ideal. Twenty minutes past four, sharp, and here's Baby wide-eyed as a marigold. Look at this, will you? At the time when all decent people are just going to bed, I must wake up. There's no way things can ever come out even, under this system. This is as rank as injustice is ever likely to get. This is what brings about hatred and bloodshed, that's what *this* does.

Yes, and you want to know what got me into this mess? Going to bed at ten o'clock, that's what. That spells ruin. T-e-n-space-o-apostrophe-c-l-o-c-k: ruin. Early to bed, and you'll wish you were dead. Bed before eleven, nuts before seven. Bed before morning, sailors give warning. Ten o'clock, after a quiet evening of reading. Reading – there's an institution for you. Why, I'd turn on the light and read, right this minute, if reading weren't what contributed toward driving me here. I'll show it. God, the bitter misery that reading works in this world! Everybody knows that – everybody who *is* everybody. All the best minds have been off reading for years. Look at the swing La Rochefoucauld took at it. He said that if nobody had ever learned to read, very few people would be in love. There was a man for you, and that's what *he* thought of it. Good for you, La Rochefoucauld; nice going, boy. I wish I'd never learned to read. I wish I'd never learned to take off my clothes. Then I wouldn't have been caught in this jam at half-past four in the morning. If nobody had ever learned to undress, very few people would be in love. No, his is better. Oh, well, it's a man's world.

La Rochefoucauld, indeed, lying quiet as a mouse, and me tossing and turning here! This is no time to be getting all steamed up about La Rochefoucauld. It's only a question of minutes before I'm going to be pretty darned good and sick of La Rochefoucauld, once and for all. La Rochefoucauld this and La Rochefoucauld that. Yes, well, let me tell you that if nobody had ever learned to quote, very few people would be in love with La Rochefoucauld. I bet you I don't know ten souls who read him without a middleman. People pick up those scholarly little essays that start off 'Was it not that lovable old cynic, La Rochefoucauld, who said . . .' and then they go around claiming to know the master backwards. Pack of illiterates, that's all they are. All right, let them keep their La Rochefoucauld, and see if I care. I'll stick to La Fontaine. Only I'd be better company if I could quit thinking that La Fontaine married Alfred Lunt.

I don't know what I'm doing mucking about with a lot of French authors at this hour, anyway. First thing you know, I'll be reciting *Fleurs du Mal* to myself, and then I'll be little more good to anybody. And I'll stay off Verlaine too; he was always chasing Rimbauds. A person would be better off with La Rochefoucauld, even. Oh, damn La Rochefoucauld. The big Frog. I'll thank him to keep out of my head. What's he doing there, anyhow? What's La Rochefoucauld to me, or he to Hecuba? Why, I don't even know the man's first name, that's how close I ever was to *him*. What am I supposed to be, a hostess to La Rochefoucauld? That's what *he* thinks. Sez he. Well, he's only wasting his time, hanging around here. I can't help him. The only other thing I can remember his saying is that there is always something a little pleasing to us in the misfortunes of even our dearest friends. That cleans me all up with Monsieur La Rochefoucauld. *Maintenant c'est fini, ça.*

Dearest friends. A sweet lot of dearest friends *I've* got. All of them lying in swinish stupors, while I'm practically up and about. All of them stretched sodden through these, the fairest hours of the day, when man should be at his most productive. Produce, produce, produce, for I tell you the night is coming. Carlyle said that. Yes, and a fine one *he* was, to go shooting off his face on production. *Oh*, Thomas Car*li*-yill, what *I* know about *you*-oo! No, that will be enough of that. I'm not going to start fretting about Carlyle, at this stage of the game. What did he ever do that was so great, besides founding a college for Indians? (That one ought to make him spin.) Let him keep his face out of this, if he knows what's good for him. I've got enough trouble with that lovable old cynic, La Rochefoucauld – him and the misfortunes of his dearest friends!

The first thing I've got to do is to get out and whip me up a complete new set of dearest friends; that's the first thing. Everything else can wait. And will somebody please kindly be so good as to inform me how I am ever going to meet up with any new people when my entire scheme of living is out of joint – when I'm the only living being awake while the rest of the world lies sleeping? I've got to get this thing adjusted. I must try to get back to sleep right now. I've got to conform to the rotten little standards of this sluggard civilization. People needn't feel that they have to change their ruinous habits and come my way. Oh, no, no, no, indeed. Not at all. I'll go theirs. If that isn't the woman of it for you! Always having to do what somebody else wants, like it or not. Never able to murmur a suggestion of her own.

And what suggestion has anyone to murmur as to how I am going to drift lightly back to slumber? Here I am, awake as high noon what with all this milling and pitching around with La Rochefoucauld. I really can't be expected to drop everything and start counting sheep, at my age. I hate sheep. Untender it may be in me, but all my life I've hated sheep. It amounts to a phobia, the way I hate them. I can tell the minute there's one in the room. They needn't think that I am going to lie here in the dark and count their unpleasant little faces for them; I wouldn't do it if I didn't fall asleep again until the middle of next August. Suppose they never get counted – what's the worst that can happen? If the number of imaginary sheep in this world remains a matter of guesswork, who is richer or poorer for it? No, sir; *I'm* not their scorekeeper. Let them count themselves, if they're so crazy mad after mathematics. Let them do their own dirty work. Coming around here, at this time of day, and asking me to count them! And not even *real* sheep, at that. Why, it's the most preposterous thing I ever heard in my life.

But there must be *something* I could count. Let's see. No, I already know by heart how many fingers I have. I could count my bills, I suppose. I could count the things I didn't do yesterday that I should have done. I could count the things I should do today that I'm not going to do. I'm never going to accomplish anything; that's perfectly clear to me. I'm never going to be famous. My name will never be writ large on the roster of Those Who Do Things. I don't do anything. Not one single thing. I used to bite my nails, but I don't even do that any more. I don't amount to the powder to blow me to hell. I've turned out to be nothing but a bit of flotsam. Flotsam and leave'em – that's me from now on. Oh, it's all terrible.

Well. This way lies galloping melancholia. Maybe it's because this is the zero hour. This is the time the swooning soul hangs pendant and vertiginous between the new day and the old, nor dares confront the one or summon back the other. This is the time when all things, known and hidden, are iron to weight the spirit; when all ways, traveled or virgin, fall away from the stumbling feet, when all before the straining eyes is black. Blackness now, everywhere is blackness. This is the time of abomination, the dreadful hour of the victorious dark. For it is always darkest – Was it not that lovable old cynic, La Rochefoucauld, who said it is always darkest before the deluge?

There. Now you see, don't you? Here we are again, practically back where we started. La Rochefoucauld, we are here. Ah, come on, son – how about your going your way and letting me go mine? I've got my work cut out for me right here; I've got all this sleeping to do. Think how I am going to look by daylight if this keeps up. I'll be a seamy sight for all those rested, clear-eyed, fresh-faced dearest friends of mine – the rats! My *dear*, whatever have you been doing; I thought you were so good lately. Oh, I was helling around with La Rochefoucauld till all hours; we couldn't stop laughing about your misfortunes. No, this is getting too thick, really. It isn't right to have this happen to a person, just because she went to bed at ten o'clock once in her life. Honest, I won't ever do it again. I'll go straight, after this. I'll never go to bed again, if I can only sleep now. If I can tear my mind away from a certain French cynic, *circa* 1650, and slip into lovely oblivion. 1650. I bet I look as if I'd been awake since then.

How do people go to sleep? I'm afraid I've lost the knack. I might try busting myself smartly over the temple with the night-light. I might repeat to myself, slowly and soothingly, a list of quotations beautiful from minds profound; if I can remember any of the damn things. That might do it. And it ought effectually to bar that visiting foreigner that's been hanging around ever since twenty minutes past four. Yes, that's what I'll do. Only wait till I turn the pillow; it feels as if La Rochefoucauld had crawled inside the slip.

Now let's see – where shall we start? Why – er – let's see. Oh, yes, I know one. This above all, to thine own self be true and it must follow, as the night the day, thou canst not then be false to any man. Now they're off. And once they get started, they ought to come like hot cakes. Let's see. Ah, what avail the sceptered race and what the form divine, when every virtue, every grace, Rose Aylmer, all were thine. Let's see. They also serve who only stand and wait. If Winter comes, can Spring be far behind? Lilies that fester smell far worse than weeds. Silent upon a peak in Darien. Mrs Porter and her daughter wash their feet in soda-water. And Agatha's Arth is a hug-the-hearth, but my true love is false. Why did you die when lambs were cropping, you should have died when apples were dropping. Shall be together, breathe and ride, so one day more am I deified, who knows but the world will end tonight. And he shall hear the stroke of eight and not the stroke of nine. They are not long, the weeping and the laughter; love and desire and hate I think will have no portion in us after we pass the gate. But none, I think, do there embrace. I think that I shall never see a poem lovely as a tree. I think I will not hang myself today. Ay tank Ay go home now.

Let's see. Solitude is the safeguard of mediocrity and the stern companion of genius. Consistency is the hobgoblin of little minds. Something is emotion remembered in tranquillity. A cynic is one who knows the price of everything and the value of nothing. That lovable old cynic is one who – oops, there's King Charles's head again. I've got to watch myself. Let's see. Circumstantial evidence is a trout in the milk. Any stigma will do to beat a dogma. If you would learn what God thinks about money, you have only to look at those to whom He has given it. If nobody had ever learned to read, very few people –

All right. That fixes it. I throw in the towel right now. I know when I'm licked. There'll be no more of this nonsense; I'm going to turn on the light and read my head off. Till the next ten o'clock, if I feel like it. And what does La Rochefoucauld want to make of that? Oh, he *will*, eh? Yes, he will! He and who else? La Rochefoucauld and *what* very few people?

Glory in the Daytime

Mr Murdock was one who carried no enthusiasm whatever for plays and their players, and that was too bad, for they meant so much to little Mrs Murdock. Always she had been in a state of devout excitement over the luminous, free, passionate elect who serve the theater. And always she had done her wistful worshiping, along with the multitudes, at the great public altars. It is true that once, when she was a particularly little girl, love had impelled her to write Miss Maude Adams a letter beginning 'Dearest Peter,' and she had received from Miss Adams a miniature thimble inscribed 'A kiss from Peter Pan.' (That was a day!) And once, when her mother had taken her holiday shopping, a limousine door was held open and there had passed her, as close as *that*, a wonder of sable and violets and round red curls that seemed to tinkle on the air; so, forever after, she was as good as certain that she had been not a foot away from Miss Billie Burke. But until some three years after her marriage, these had remained her only personal experiences with the people of the lights and the glory.

Then it turned out that Miss Noyes, new come to little Mrs Murdock's own bridge club, knew an actress. She actually knew an actress: the way you and I know collectors of recipes and members of garden clubs and amateurs of needlepoint.

The name of the actress was Lily Wynton, and it was famous. She was tall and slow and silvery; often she appeared in the role of a duchess, or of a Lady Pam or an Honorable Moira. Critics recurrently referred to her as 'that great lady of our stage'. Mrs Murdock had attended, over years, matinee performances of the Wynton successes. And she had no more thought that she would one day have opportunity to meet Lily Wynton face to face than she had thought – well, than she had thought of flying!

Yet it was not astounding that Miss Noyes should walk at ease among the glamorous. Miss Noyes was full of depths and mystery, and she could talk with a cigarette still between her lips. She was always doing something difficult, like designing her own pajamas, or reading Proust, or modeling torsos in plasticine. She played excellent bridge. She liked little Mrs Murdock. 'Tiny one,' she called her.

'How's for coming to tea tomorrow, tiny one? Lily

Wynton's going to drop up,' she said, at a therefore memorable meeting of the bridge club. 'You might like to meet her.'

The words fell so easily that she could not have realized their weight. Lily Wynton was coming to tea. Mrs Murdock might like to meet her. Little Mrs Murdock walked home through the early dark, and stars sang in the sky above her.

Mr Murdock was already at home when she arrived. It required but a glance to tell that for him there had been no singing stars that evening in the heavens. He sat with his newspaper opened at the financial page, and bitterness had its way with his soul. It was not the time to cry happily to him of the impending hospitalities of Miss Noyes; not the time, that is, if one anticipated exclamatory sympathy. Mr Murdock did not like Miss Noyes. When pressed for a reason, he replied that he just plain didn't like her. Occasionally he added, with a sweep that might have commanded a certain admiration, that all those women made him sick. Usually, when she told him of the temperate activities of the bridge club meetings, Mrs Murdock kept any mention of Miss Noyes's name from the accounts. She had found that this omission made for a more agreeable evening. But now she was caught in such a sparkling swirl of excitement that she had scarcely kissed him before she was off on her story.

'Oh, Jim,' she cried. 'Oh, what do you think! Hallie Noyes asked me to tea tomorrow to meet Lily Wynton!'

'Who's Lily Wynton?' he said.

'Ah, Jim,' she said. 'Ah, really, Jim. Who's Lily Wynton! Who's Greta Garbo, I suppose!'

'She some actress or something?' he said.

Mrs Murdock's shoulders sagged. 'Yes, Jim,' she said. 'Yes. Lily Wynton's an actress.'

She picked up her purse and started slowly toward the door. But before she had taken three steps, she was again caught up in her sparkling swirl. She turned to him, and her eyes were shining.

'Honestly,' she said, 'it was the funniest thing you ever heard in your life. We'd just finished the last rubber – oh, I forgot to tell you, I won three dollars, isn't that pretty good for me? – and Hallie Noyes said to me, "Come on in to tea tomorrow. Lily Wynton's going to drop up," she said. Just like that, she said it. Just as if it was anybody.'

'Drop up?' he said. 'How can you drop *up*?'

'Honestly, I don't know what I said when she asked me,' Mrs Murdock said. 'I suppose I said I'd love to – I guess I must have. But I was so simply – Well, you know how I've always felt about Lily Wynton. Why, when I was a little girl, I used to collect her pictures. And I've seen her in, oh, everything she's ever been in, I should think, and I've read every word about her, and interviews and all. Really and truly, when I think of *meeting* her – Oh, I'll simply die. What on earth shall I say to her?'

'You might ask her how she'd like to try dropping down, for a change,' Mr Murdock said.

'All right, Jim,' Mrs Murdock said. 'If that's the way you want to be.'

Wearily she went toward the door, and this time she reached it before she turned to him. There were no lights in her eyes.

'It – it isn't so awfully nice,' she said, 'to spoil somebody's pleasure in something. I was so thrilled about this. You don't see what it is to me, to meet Lily Wynton. To meet somebody like that, and see what they're like, and hear what they say, and maybe get to know them. People like that mean – well, they mean something different to me. They're not like this. They're not like me. Who do I ever see? What do I ever hear? All my whole life, I've wanted to know – I've almost prayed that some day I could meet – Well. All right, Jim.'

She went out, and on to her bedroom.

Mr Murdock was left with only his newspaper and his bitterness for company. But he spoke aloud.

' "Drop up!" ' he said. ' "Drop up," for God's sake!'

The Murdocks dined, not in silence, but in pronounced quiet. There was something straitened about Mr Murdock's stillness; but little Mrs Murdock's was the sweet, far quiet of one given over to dreams. She had forgotten her weary words to her husband, she had passed through her excitement and her disappointment. Luxuriously she floated on innocent visions of days after the morrow. She heard her own voice in future conversations . . .

I saw Lily Wynton at Hallie's the other day, and she was telling me all about her new play – no, I'm terribly sorry, but it's a secret, I promised her I wouldn't tell anyone the name of it . . . Lily Wynton dropped up to tea yesterday, and we just got to talking, and she told me the most interesting things about her life; she said she'd never dreamed of telling them to anyone else . . . Why, I'd love to come, but I promised to have lunch with Lily Wynton . . . I had a long, long letter from Lily Wynton . . . Lily Wynton called me up this morning . . . Whenever I feel blue, I just go and have a talk with Lily Wynton, and then I'm all right again . . . Lily Wynton told me . . . Lily Wynton and I . . . 'Lily,' I said to her . . .

The next morning, Mr Murdock had left for his office before Mrs Murdock rose. This had happened several times before, but not often. Mrs Murdock felt a little queer about it. Then she told herself that it was probably just as well. Then she forgot all about it, and gave her mind to the selection of a costume suitable to the afternoon's event. Deeply she felt that her small wardrobe included no dress adequate to the occasion: for, of course, such an occasion had never before arisen. She finally decided upon a frock of dark blue serge with fluted white muslin about the neck and wrists. It was her style, that was the most she could say for it. And that was all she could say for herself. Blue serge and little white ruffles – that was she.

The very becomingness of the dress lowered her spirits. A nobody's frock, worn by a nobody. She blushed and went hot when she recalled the dreams she had woven the night before, the mad visions of intimacy, of equality with Lily Wynton. Timidity turned her heart liquid, and she thought of telephoning Miss Noyes and saying she had a bad cold and could not come. She steadied, when she planned a course of conduct to pursue at teatime. She would not try to say anything; if she stayed silent, she could not sound foolish. She would listen and watch and worship and then come home, stronger, braver, better for an hour she would remember proudly all her life.

Miss Noyes's living-room was done in the early modern period. There were a great many oblique lines and acute angles, zigzags of aluminum and horizontal stretches of mirror. The color scheme was sawdust and steel. No seat was more than twelve inches above the floor, no table was made of wood. It was, as has been said of larger places, all right for a visit.

Little Mrs Murdock was the first arrival. She was glad of that: no, maybe it would have been better to have come after Lily Wynton; no, maybe this was right. The maid motioned her toward the living-room, and Miss Noyes greeted her in the cool voice and the warm words that were her special combination. She wore black velvet trousers, a red cummerbund, and a white silk shirt, opened at the throat. A cigarette clung to her lower lip, and her eyes, as was her habit, were held narrow against its near smoke.

'Come in, come in, tiny one,' she said. 'Bless its little heart. Take off its little coat. Good Lord, you look easily eleven years old in that dress. Sit ye doon, here beside of me. There'll be a spot of tea in a jiff.'

Mrs Murdock sat down on the vast, perilously low divan, and, because she was never good at reclining among cushions, held her back straight. There was room for six like her, between herself and her hostess. Miss Noyes lay back with one ankle flung upon the other knee, and looked at her.

'I'm a wreck,' Miss Noyes announced. 'I was modeling like a mad thing, all night long. It's taken everything out of me. I was like a thing bewitched.'

'Oh, what were you making?' cried Mrs Murdock.

'Oh, Eve,' Miss Noyes said. 'I always do Eve. What else is there to do? You must come pose for me some time, tiny one. You'd be nice to do. Ye-es, you'd be very nice to do. My tiny one.'

'Why, I –' Mrs Murdock said, and stopped. 'Thank you very much, though,' she said.

'I wonder where Lily is,' Miss Noyes said. 'She said she'd be here early – well, she always says that. You'll adore her, tiny one. She's really rare. She's a real person. And she's been through perfect hell. God, what a time she's had!'

'Ah, what's been the matter?' said Mrs Murdock.

'Men,' Miss Noyes said. 'Men. She never had a man that wasn't a louse.' Gloomily she stared at the toe of her flat-heeled patent leather pump. 'A pack of lice, always. All of them. Leave her for the first little floozie that comes along.'

'But –' Mrs Murdock began. No, she couldn't have heard right. How could it be right? Lily Wynton was a great actress. A great actress meant romance. Romance meant Grand Dukes and Crown Princes and diplomats touched with gray at the temples and lean, bronzed, reckless Younger Sons. It meant pearls and emeralds and chinchilla and rubies red as the blood that was shed for them. It meant a grim-faced boy sitting in the fearful Indian midnight, beneath the dreary whirring of the *punkahs*, writing a letter to the lady he had seen but once; writing his poor heart out, before he turned to the service revolver that lay beside him on the table. It meant a golden-locked poet, floating face downward in the sea, and in his pocket his last great sonnet to the lady of ivory. It meant brave, beautiful men, living and dying for the lady who was the pale bride of art, whose eyes and heart were soft with only compassion for them.

A pack of lice. Crawling after little floozies; whom Mrs Murdock swiftly and hazily pictured as rather like ants.

'But –' said little Mrs Murdock.

'She gave them all her money,' Miss Noyes said. 'She always did. Or if she didn't, they took it anyway. Took every cent she had, and then spat in her face. Well, maybe I'm teaching her a little bit of sense now. Oh, there's the bell – that'll be Lily. No, sit ye doon, tiny one. You belong there.'

Miss Noyes rose and made for the archway that separated the living-room from the hall. As she passed Mrs Murdock, she stooped suddenly, cupped her guest's round chin, and quickly, lightly kissed her mouth.

'Don't tell Lily,' she murmured, very low.

Mrs Murdock puzzled. Don't tell Lily what? Could Hallie Noyes think that she might babble to *the* Lily Wynton of these strange confidences about the actress's life? Or did she mean – But she had no more time for puzzling. Lily Wynton stood in the archway. There she stood, one hand resting on the wooden molding and her body swayed toward it, exactly as she stood for her third-act entrance of her latest play, and for a like half-minute.

You would have known her anywhere, Mrs Murdock thought. Oh, yes, anywhere. Or at least you would have exclaimed, 'That woman looks something like Lily Wynton.' For she was somehow different in the day-light. Her figure looked heavier, thicker, and her face – there was so much of her face that the surplus sagged from the strong, fine bones. And her eyes, those famous dark, liquid eyes. They were dark, yes, and certainly liquid, but they were set in little hammocks of folded flesh, and seemed to be set but loosely, so readily did they roll. Their whites, that were visible all around the irises, were threaded with tiny scarlet veins.

'I suppose footlights are an awful strain on their eyes,' thought little Mrs Murdock.

Lily Wynton wore, just as she should have, black satin and sables, and long white gloves were wrinkled luxuriously about her wrists. But there were delicate streaks of grime in the folds of her gloves, and down the shining length of her gown there were small, irregularly shaped dull patches; bits of food or drops of drink, or perhaps both, sometime must have slipped their carriers and found brief sanctuary there. Her hat – oh, her hat. It was romance, it was mystery, it was strange, sweet sorrow; it was Lily Wynton's hat, of all the world, and no other could dare it. Black it was, and tilted, and a great, soft plume drooped from it to follow her cheek and curl across her throat. Beneath it, her hair had the various hues of neglected brass. But, oh, her hat.

'Darling!' cried Miss Noyes.

'Angel,' said Lily Wynton. 'My sweet.'

It was that voice. It was that deep, soft, glowing voice. 'Like purple velvet,' someone had written. Mrs Murdock's heart beat visibly.

Lily Wynton cast herself upon the steep bosom of her hostess, and murmured there. Across Miss Noyes's shoulder she caught sight of little Mrs Murdock.

'And who is this?' she said. She disengaged herself.

'That's my tiny one,' Miss Noyes said. 'Mrs Murdock.'

'What a clever little face,' said Lily Wynton. 'Clever, clever little face. What does she do, sweet Hallie? I'm sure she writes, doesn't she? Yes, I can feel it. She writes beautiful, beautiful words. Don't you, child?'

'Oh, no, really I –' Mrs Murdock said.

'And you must write me a play,' said Lily Wynton. 'A beautiful, beautiful play. And I will play in it, over and over the world, until I am a very, very old lady. And then I will die. But I will never be forgotten, because of the years I played in your beautiful, beautiful play.'

She moved across the room. There was a slight hesitancy, a seeming insecurity, in her step, and when she would have sunk into a chair, she began to sink two inches, perhaps, to its right. But she swayed just in time in her descent, and was safe.

'To write,' she said, smiling sadly at Mrs Murdock, 'to write. And such a little thing, for such a big gift. Oh, the privilege of it. But the anguish of it, too. The agony.'

'But, you see, I –' said little Mrs Murdock.

'Tiny one doesn't write, Lily,' Miss Noyes said. She threw herself back upon the divan. 'She's a museum piece. She's a devoted wife.'

'A wife!' Lily Wynton said. 'A wife. Your first marriage, child?'

'Oh, yes,' said Mrs Murdock.

'How sweet,' Lily Wynton said. 'How sweet, sweet, sweet. Tell me, child, do you love him very, very much?'

'Why, I –' said little Mrs Murdock, and blushed. 'I've been married for ages,' she said.

'You love him,' Lily Wynton said. 'You love him. And is it sweet to go to bed with him?'

'Oh –' said Mrs Murdock, and blushed till it hurt.

'The first marriage,' Lily Wynton said. 'Youth, youth. Yes, when I was your age I used to marry, too. Oh, treasure your love, child, guard it, live in it. Laugh and dance in the love of your man. Until you find out what he's really like.'

There came a sudden visitation upon her. Her shoulders jerked upward, her cheeks puffed, her eyes sought to start from their hammocks. For a moment she sat thus, then slowly all subsided into place. She lay back in her chair, tenderly patting her chest. She shook her head sadly, and there was grieved wonder in the look with which she held Mrs Murdock.

'Gas,' said Lily Wynton, in the famous voice. 'Gas. Nobody knows what I suffer from it.'

'Oh, I'm so sorry,' Mrs Murdock said. 'Is there anything –'

'Nothing,' Lily Wynton said. 'There is nothing. There is nothing that can be done for it. I've been everywhere.'

'How's for a spot of tea, perhaps?' Miss Noyes said. 'It might help.' She turned her face toward the archway and lifted up her voice. 'Mary! Where the hell's the tea?'

'You don't know,' Lily Wynton said, with her grieved eyes fixed on Mrs Murdock, 'you don't know what stomach distress is. You can never, never know, unless you're a stomach sufferer yourself. I've been one for years. Years and years and years.'

'I'm terribly sorry,' Mrs Murdock said.

'Nobody knows the anguish,' Lily Wynton said. 'The agony.'

The maid appeared, bearing a triangular tray upon which was set an heroic-sized tea service of bright white china, each piece a hectagon. She set it down on a table within the long reach of Miss Noyes and retired, as she had come, bashfully.

'Sweet Hallie,' Lily Wynton said, 'my sweet. Tea – I adore it. I worship it. But my distress turns it to gall and wormwood in me. Gall and wormwood. For hours, I should have no peace. Let me have a little, tiny bit of your beautiful, beautiful brandy, instead.'

'You really think you should, darling?' Miss Noyes said. 'You know –'

'My angel,' said Lily Wynton, 'it's the only thing for acidity.'

'Well,' Miss Noyes said. 'But do remember you've got a performance tonight.' Again she hurled her voice at the archway. 'Mary! Bring the brandy and a lot of soda and ice and things.'

'Oh, no, my saint,' Lily Wynton said. 'No, no, sweet Hallie. Soda and ice are rank poison to me. Do you want to freeze my poor, weak stomach? Do you want to kill poor, poor Lily?'

'Mary!' roared Miss Noyes. 'Just bring the brandy and a glass.' She turned to little Mrs Murdock. 'How's for your tea, tiny one? Cream? Lemon?'

'Cream, if I may, please,' Mrs Murdock said. 'And two lumps of sugar, please, if I may.'

'Oh, youth, youth,' Lily Wynton said. 'Youth and love.'

The maid returned with an octagonal tray supporting a decanter of brandy and a wide, squat, heavy glass. Her head twisted on her neck in a spasm of diffidence.

'Just pour it for me, will you, my dear?' said Lily Wynton. 'Thank you. And leave the pretty, pretty decanter here, on this enchanting little table. Thank you. You're so good to me.'

The maid vanished, fluttering. Lily Wynton lay back in her chair, holding in her gloved hand the wide, squat glass, colored brown to the brim. Little Mrs Murdock lowered her eyes to her teacup, carefully carried it to her lips, sipped, and replaced it on its saucer. When she raised her eyes, Lily Wynton lay back in her chair, holding in her gloved hand the wide, squat, colorless glass.

'My life,' Lily Wynton said, slowly, 'is a mess. A stinking mess. It always has been, and it always will be. Until I am a very, very old lady. Ah, little Clever-Face, you writers don't know what struggle is.'

'But really I'm not –' said Mrs Murdock.

'To write,' Lily Wynton said. 'To write. To set one word beautifully beside another word. The privilege of it. The blessed, blessed peace of it. Oh, for quiet, for rest. But do you think those cheap bastards would close that play while it's doing a nickel's worth of business? Oh, no. Tired as I am, sick as I am, I must drag along. Oh, child, child, guard your precious gift. Give thanks for it. It is the greatest thing of all. It is the only thing. To write.'

'Darling, I told you tiny one doesn't write,' said Miss Noyes. 'How's for making more sense? She's a wife.'

'Ah, yes, she told me. She told me she had perfect, passionate love,' Lily Wynton said. 'Young love. It is the greatest thing. It is the only thing.' She grasped the decanter; and again the squat glass was brown to the brim.

'What time did you start today, darling?' said Miss Noyes.

'Oh, don't scold me, sweet love,' Lily Wynton said.

'Lily hasn't been naughty. Her wuzzunt naughty dirl 't all. I didn't get up until late, late, late. And though I parched, though I burned, I didn't have a drink until after my breakfast. "It is for Hallie," I said.' She raised the glass to her mouth, tilted it, and brought it away, colorless.

'Good Lord, Lily,' Miss Noyes said. 'Watch yourself. You've got to walk on that stage tonight, my girl.'

'All the world's a stage,' said Lily Wynton. 'And all the men and women merely players. They have their entrance and their exitses, and each man in his time plays many parts, his act being seven ages. At first, the infant, mewling and puking –'

'How's the play doing?' Miss Noyes said.

'Oh, lousily,' Lily Wynton said. 'Lousily, lousily, lousily. But what isn't? What isn't, in this terrible, terrible world? Answer me that.' She reached for the decanter.

'Lily, listen,' said Miss Noyes. 'Stop that. Do you hear?'

'Please, sweet Hallie,' Lily Wynton said. 'Pretty please. Poor, poor Lily.'

'Do you want me to do what I had to do last time?' Miss Noyes said. 'Do you want me to strike you, in front of tiny one, here?'

Lily Wynton drew herself high. 'You do not realize,' she said, icily, 'what acidity is.' She filled the glass and held it, regarding it as though through a lorgnon. Suddenly her manner changed, and she looked up and smiled at little Mrs Murdock.

'You must let me read it,' she said. 'You mustn't be so modest.'

'Read –?' said little Mrs Murdock.

'Your play,' Lily Wynton said. 'Your beautiful, beautiful play. Don't think I am too busy. I always have time. I have time for everything. Oh, my God, I have to go to the dentist tomorrow. Oh, the suffering I have gone through with my teeth. Look!' She set down her glass, inserted a gloved forefinger in the corner of her mouth, and dragged it to the side. 'Oogh!' she insisted. 'Oogh!'

Mrs Murdock craned her neck shyly, and caught a glimpse of shining gold.

'Oh, I'm so sorry,' she said.

'As wah ee id a me ass ime,' Lily Wynton said. She took away her forefinger and let her mouth resume its shape. 'That's what he did to me last time,' she repeated. 'The anguish of it. The agony. Do you suffer with your teeth, little Clever-Face?'

'Why, I'm afraid I've been awfully lucky,' Mrs Murdock said. 'I –'

'You don't know,' Lily Wynton said. 'Nobody knows what it is. You writers – you don't know.' She took up her glass, sighed over it, and drained it.

'Well,' Miss Noyes said. 'Go ahead and pass out, then, darling. You'll have time for a sleep before the theater.'

'To sleep,' Lily Wynton said. 'To sleep, perchance to dream. The privilege of it. Oh, Hallie, sweet, sweet Hallie, poor Lily feels so terrible. Rub my head for me, angel. Help me.'

'I'll go get the Eau de Cologne,' Miss Noyes said. She left the room lightly patting Mrs Murdock's knee as she passed her. Lily Wynton lay in her chair and closed her famous eyes.

'To sleep,' she said. 'To sleep, perchance to dream.'

'I'm afraid,' little Mrs Murdock began. 'I'm afraid,' she said, 'I really must be going home. I'm afraid I didn't realize how awfully late it was.'

'Yes, go, child,' Lily Wynton said. She did not open her eyes. 'Go to him. Go to him, live in him, love him. Stay with him always. But when he starts bringing them into the house – get out.'

'I'm afraid – I'm afraid I didn't quite understand,' Mrs Murdock said.

'When he starts bringing his fancy women into the house,' Lily Wynton said. 'You must have pride, then. You must go. I always did. But it was always too late then. They'd got all my money. That's all they want, marry them or not. They say it's love, but it isn't. Love is the only thing. Treasure your love, child. Go back to him. Go to bed with him. It's the only thing. And your beautiful, beautiful play.'

'Oh, dear,' said little Mrs Murdock. 'I – I'm afraid it's really terribly late.'

There was only the sound of rhythmic breathing from the chair where Lily Wynton lay. The purple voice rolled along the air no longer.

Little Mrs Murdock stole to the chair upon which she had left her coat. Carefully she smoothed her white muslin frills, so that they would be fresh beneath the jacket. She felt a tenderness for her frock; she wanted to protect it. Blue serge and little ruffles – they were her own.

When she reached the outer door of Miss Noyes's apartment, she stopped a moment and her manners conquered her. Bravely she called in the direction of Miss Noyes's bedroom.

'Good-by, Miss Noyes,' she said. 'I've simply got to run. I didn't realize it was so late. I had a lovely time – thank you ever so much.'

'Oh, good-by, tiny one,' Miss Noyes called. 'Sorry Lily went by-by. Don't mind her – she's really a real person. I'll call you up, tiny one. I want to see you. Now where's that damned Cologne?'

'Thank you ever so much,' Mrs Murdock said. She let herself out of the apartment.

Little Mrs Murdock walked homeward, through the clustering dark. Her mind was busy, but not with memories of Lily Wynton. She thought of Jim; Jim, who had left for his office before she had arisen that morning, Jim, whom she had not kissed good-by. Darling Jim. There were no others born like him. Funny Jim, stiff and cross and silent; but only because he knew so much. Only because he knew the silliness of seeking afar for the glamour and beauty and romance of living. When they were right at home all the time, she thought. Like the Blue Bird, thought little Mrs Murdock.

Darling Jim. Mrs Murdock turned in her course, and entered an enormous shop where the most delicate and esoteric of foods were sold for heavy sums. Jim liked red caviar. Mrs Murdock bought a jar of the shiny, glutinous eggs. They would have cocktails that night, though they had no guests, and the red caviar would be served with them for a surprise, and it would be a little, secret party to celebrate her return to contentment with her Jim, a party to mark her happy renunciation of all the glory of the world. She bought, too, a large, foreign cheese. It would give a needed touch to dinner. Mrs Murdock had not given much attention to ordering dinner, that morning. 'Oh, anything you want, Signe,' she had said to the maid. She did not want to think of that. She went on home with her packages.

Mr Murdock was already there when she arrived. He was sitting with his newspaper opened to the financial page. Little Mrs Murdock ran in to him with her eyes a-light. It is too bad that the light in a person's eyes is only the light in a person's eyes, and you cannot tell at a look what causes it. You do not know if it is excitement about you, or about something else. The evening before, Mrs Murdock had run in to Mr Murdock with her eyes a-light.

'Oh, hello,' he said to her. He looked back at his paper, and kept his eyes there. 'What did you do? Did you drop up to Hank Noyes's?'

Little Mrs Murdock stopped right where she was.

'You know perfectly well, Jim,' she said, 'that Hallie Noyes's first name is Hallie.'

'It's Hank to me,' he said. 'Hank or Bill. Did what's-her-name show up? I mean drop up. Pardon me.'

'To whom are you referring?' said Mrs Murdock, perfectly.

'What's-her-name,' Mr Murdock said. 'The movie star.'

'If you mean Lily Wynton,' Mrs Murdock said, 'she is not a movie star. She is an actress. She is a great actress.'

'Well, did she drop up?' he said.

Mrs Murdock's shoulders sagged. 'Yes,' she said. 'Yes, she was there, Jim.'

'I suppose you're going on the stage now,' he said.

'Ah, Jim,' Mrs Murdock said. 'Ah, Jim, please. I'm not sorry at all I went to Hallie Noyes's today. It was – it was a real experience to meet Lily Wynton. Something I'll remember all my life.'

'What did she do?' Mr Murdock said. 'Hang by her feet?'

'She did no such thing!' Mrs Murdock said. 'She recited Shakespeare, if you want to know.'

'Oh, my God,' Mr Murdock said. 'That must have been great.'

'All right, Jim,' Mrs Murdock said. 'If that's the way you want to be.'

Wearily she left the room and went down the hall. She stopped at the pantry door, pushed it open, and spoke to the pleasant little maid.

'Oh, Signe,' she said. 'Oh, good evening, Signe. Put these things somewhere, will you? I got them on the way home. I thought we might have them some time.'

Wearily little Mrs Murdock went on down the hall to her bedroom.

Lolita

Mrs Ewing was a short woman who accepted the obligation borne by so many short women to make up in vivacity what they lack in number of inches from the ground. She was a creature of little pats and prods, little crinklings of the eyes and wrinklings of the nose, little runs and ripples of speech and movement, little spirals of laughter. Whenever Mrs Ewing entered a place, all stillness left it.

Her age was a matter of guesswork, save for those who had been at school with her. For herself, she declared that she paid no attention to her birthdays – didn't give a hoot about them; and it is true that when you have amassed several dozen of the same sort of thing, it loses that rarity which is the excitement of collectors. In the summertime, she wore little cotton play suits, though her only game was bridge, and short socks, revealing the veins along the backs of her legs. For winter, she chose frocks of audible taffeta, frilled and frilled again, and jackets made of the skins of the less-sought-after lower animals. Often, of an evening, she tied a pale ribbon in her hair. Through shimmering heat or stabbing wind Mrs Ewing trudged to her hairdresser's; her locks had been so frequently and so drastically brightened and curled that to caress them, one felt, would be rather like running one's fingers through julienne potatoes. She decorated her small, square face in a manner not unusual among ladies of the South and the Southwest, powdering the nose and chin sharp white and applying circles of rouge to the cheeks. Seen from an end of a long, softly lighted room, Mrs Ewing was a pretty woman.

She had long been a widowed lady. Even before her widowhood, she and Mr Ewing had lived separately, while the sympathy of the town dwelt with her. She had dallied with the notion of divorce, for it is well known that the thought, much less the presence, of a merry divorcee sets gentlemen to pawing the ground and snorting. But before her plans took form, Mr Ewing, always a devout believer in the doctrine of one more for the road, was killed in an automobile accident. Still, a widow, too, a soft little widow, has repute the world over for causing the hearts of gentlemen to beat warm and fast. Mrs Ewing and her friends felt sure that she would marry again. Time slid on, and this did not happen.

Mrs Ewing never vaunted her lorn condition, never shut herself within the shaded chambers of bereavement. She went right along, skipping and tinkling through all the social events of the town, and no week went by without her presiding in her own house over cheerful little dinners or evenings of passionate bridge. She was always the same, and always the same to everyone, although she reached her heights when there were men present. She coquetted with the solid husbands of her friends, and with the two or three bachelors of the town, tremulous antiques pouring pills into their palms at the dinner table, she was sprightly to the verge of naughtiness. To a stranger observing her might have come the thought that Mrs Ewing was not a woman who easily abandoned hope.

Mrs Ewing had a daughter: Lolita. It is, of course, the right of parents to name their offspring what they please, yet it would sometimes be easier if they could glimpse the future and see what the little one was going to look like later on. Lolita was of no color at all; she was thin, with insistent knobs at the ends of her bones, and her hair, so fine that it seemed sparse, grew straight. There was a time when Mrs Ewing, probably hostess to fantasies about a curly-headed tot, took to wetting the child's hair severely and rolling it up on strips of rags when she went to bed. But when the strips were untied in the morning, down fell the hair again, straight as ever. All that came of the project was a series of white nights for Lolita, trying to rest her head on the hard knots of the rags. So the whole thing was given up, and her hair hung as it must thereafter. In her early days at school, the little boys would chase her around the schoolyard at recess, snatching at the limp strands and crying, 'Oh, Lolita, give us a curl, willya? Ah, Lolita, give us one of your pretty curls!' The little girls, her little friends, would gather in a group to watch and say 'Oo, aren't they terrible?' and press their hands against their mouths to control their giggles.

Mrs Ewing was always her own sparkling self with her daughter, but her friends, mothers of born belles, tried to imagine themselves in her place and their hearts ached for her. Gallant in their own way, they found cases to relate to her, cases of girls who went through periods of being plain and then turned suddenly into dazzling beauties; some of the more scholarly brought up references to the story of the ugly duckling. But Lolita passed through young girlhood and came of age and the only difference in her was that she was taller.

The friends did not dislike Lolita. They spoke sweetly to her and when she was not present always inquired of her mother about her, although knowing there would be no news. Their exasperation was not with her but with the Fates, who had foisted upon Mrs Ewing that pale gawk – one, moreover, with no spirit, with never a word to say for herself. For Lolita was quiet, so quiet that often you would not realize she was in the room, until the light shone on her glasses. There was nothing to do about it; there were no hopeful anecdotes to cover the condition. The friends, thinking of their own winging, twittering young, sighed again for Mrs Ewing.

There were no beaux draped along the railing of the Ewing porch in the evening; no young male voices asked for Lolita over the telephone. At first seldom, then not at all, did the other girls ask her to their parties. This was no mark of dislike; it was only that it was difficult to bear her in mind, since school was done with for all of them and they no longer saw her daily. Mrs Ewing always had her present at her own little soirees, though the Lord knew she added nothing to them, and, dauntless, took her along to the public events attended by both old and young, festivals for the benefit of church or charity or civic embellishment. Even when brought into such festivities, Lolita would find a corner and stay there in her quiet. Her mother would call to her across the big public room, carolling high and clear above the social clatter: 'Well, come on there, little old Miss Stick-in-the-Mud! Get up on your feet and start mixing around with people!' Lolita would only smile and stay where she was, quiet as she was. There was nothing morose about her stillness. Her face, if you remembered to see it, had a look of shy welcoming, and her smile might have been set high in the tiny list of her attractions. But such attributes are valuable only when they can be quickly recognized; who has time to go searching?

It often happens in the instance of an unsought maiden daughter and a gay little mother that the girl takes over the running of the house, lifting the burden from the mother's plump shoulders. But not Lolita. She had no domestic talents. Sewing was a dark mystery to her, and if she ventured into the kitchen to attempt some simple dish, the results would be, at best, ludicrous. Nor could she set a room in pretty order. Lamps shivered, ornaments shattered, water slopped out of flower vases before her touch. Mrs Ewing never chided the girl for her clumsiness; she made jokes about it. Lolita's hands shook under railleries, and there would be only more spilled water and more splintered shepherdesses.

She could not even do the marketing successfully, although armed with a resume of the needs of the day in her mother's curly handwriting. She would arrive at the market at the proper hour, the time it was filled with women, and then seem to be unable to push her way through them. She stood aside until later arrivals had been served before she could go to the counter and murmur her wants; and so Mrs Ewing's lunch would be late. The household would have tottered if it had not been for the maid Mrs Ewing had had for years – Mardy, the super-cook, the demon cleaner. The other ladies lived uneasily with their servants, ridden with fears that they might either leave or become spoiled, but Mrs Ewing was cozy with Mardy. She was as vigorously winsome with the maid as with the better-born. They enjoyed laughing together, and right at hand was the subject of Lolita's incompetences.

Experiments palled, and finally Lolita was relieved of domestic offices. She stayed still and silent; and time went on and Mrs Ewing went on and on, bright as a bubble in the air.

Then there bloomed a certain spring, not gradually but all in a day, a season long to be referred to as the time John Marble came. The town had not before seen the like of John Marble. He looked as if he had just alighted from the chariot of the sun. He was tall and fair, and he could make no awkward move or utter no stumbling phrase. The girls lost all consciousness of the local young men, for they were nowhere as against John Marble. He was older than they – he had crossed thirty – and he must have been rich, for he had the best room at the Wade

Hampton Inn and he drove a low, narrow car with a foreign name, a thing of grace and power. More, there was about him the magic of the transitory. There were the local young men, day after day, year in, year out. But John Marble had come on some real-estate dealings for his firm, some matters of properties outside the town limits, and when his business was done, he would go back to the great, glittering city where he lived. Time pressed; excitement heightened.

Through his business John Marble met important men of the town, the fathers of daughters, and there was eager entertaining for the brilliant stranger. The girls put on the fluffiest white, and tucked bunches of pink roses in their pale-blue sashes; their curls shone and swung like bells. In the twilight they sang little songs for John Marble, and one of them had a guitar. The local young men, whose evenings hung like wet seaweed around their necks, could only go in glum groups to the bowling alley or the moving-picture theater. Though the parties in John Marble's honor slackened, for he explained that because of the demands of his business he must regret invitations, still the girls impatiently refused appointments to the local young men, and stayed at home alone on the chance of a telephone call from John Marble. They beguiled the time of waiting by sketching his profile on the telephone pad. Sometimes they threw away their training and telephoned him, even as late as ten o'clock at night. When he answered, he was softly courteous, charmingly distressed that his work kept him from being with them. Then, more and more frequently, there was no answer to their calls. The switchboard operator at the inn merely reported that Mr Marble was out.

Somehow, the difficulties in the way of coming nearer to John Marble seemed to stimulate the girls. They tossed their fragrant curls and let their laughter soar, and when they passed the Wade Hampton Inn, they less walked than sashayed. Their elders said that never in their memories had the young girls been so pretty and so spirited as they were that spring.

And with the whole townful of bright blossoms bended for his plucking, John Marble chose Lolita Ewing.

It was a courtship curiously without detail. John Marble would appear at the Ewing house in the evening, with no preliminary telephoning, and he and Lolita would sit on the porch while Mrs Ewing went out among her friends. When she returned, she shut the gate behind her with a clang, and as she started up the brick path she uttered a loud, arch '*A-hem,*' as if to warn the young people of her coming, so that they might wrench themselves one from the other. But there was never a squeal of the porch swing, never a creak of a floor board – those noises that tell tales of scurryings to new positions. The only sound was of John Marble's voice, flowing easily along; and when Mrs Ewing came up on the porch, John Marble would be lying in the swing and Lolita would be sitting in a wicker chair some five feet away from him, with her hands in her lap, and, of course, not a peep out of her. Mrs Ewing's conscience would smite her at the knowledge of John Marble's one-sided evening, and so she would sit down and toss the ball of conversation in the air and keep it there with reports of the plot of the moving picture she had seen or the hands of the bridge game in which she had taken part. When she, even she, came to a pause, John Marble would rise and explain that the next day was to be a hard one for him and so he must go. Mrs Ewing would stand at the porch steps and as he went down the path would call after him roguish instructions that he was not to do anything that she would not do.

When she and Lolita came in from the dark porch to the lighted hall, Mrs Ewing would look at her daughter in an entirely new way. Her eyes narrowed, her lips pressed together, and her mouth turned down at the corners. In silence she surveyed the girl, and still in silence not broken by even a good night, she would mount to her bedroom, and the sound of her closing door would fill the house.

The pattern of the evenings changed. John Marble no longer came to sit on the porch. He arrived in his beautiful car and took Lolita driving through the gentle dark. Mrs Ewing's thoughts followed them. They would drive out in the country, they would turn off the road to a smooth dell with thick trees to keep it secret from passersby, and there the car would stop. And what would happen then? Did they – Would they – But Mrs Ewing's thoughts could go no farther. There would come before her a picture of Lolita, and so the thoughts would be finished by her laughter.

All the days, now, she continued to regard the girl under lowered lids, and the downturn of her mouth became a habit with her, though not among her prettier ones. She seldom spoke to Lolita directly, but she still made jokes. When a wider audience was wanting, she called upon Mardy. 'Hi, Mardy!' she would cry. 'Come on in here, will you? Come in and look at her, sitting there like a queen. Little Miss High-and-Mighty, now she thinks she's caught her a beau!'

There was no announcement of engagement. It was not necessary, for the town sizzled with the news of John Marble and Lolita Ewing. There were two schools of thought as to the match: one blessed Heaven that Lolita had gained a man and the other mourned the callousness of a girl who could go away and leave her mother alone. But miracles were scarce in the annals of the town, and the first school had the more adherents. There was no time for engagement rites. John Marble's business was concluded, and he must go back. There were scarcely hours enough to make ready for the wedding.

It was a big wedding. John Marble first suggested, then stated, that his own plan would be for Lolita and him to go off alone, be married, and then start at once for New York; but Mrs Ewing paid him no heed. 'No, *sir*,' she said. 'Nobody's going to do *me* out of a great big lovely wedding!' And so nobody did.

Lolita in her bridal attire answered her mother's description of looking like nothing at all. The shiny white fabric of her gown was hostile to her colorless skin, and there was no way to pin the veil becomingly on her hair. But Mrs Ewing more than made up for her. All in pink ruffles caught up with clusters of false forget-me-nots, Mrs Ewing was at once bold sunlight and new moonlight, she was budding boughs and opening petals and little, willful breezes. She tripped through the throngs in the smilax-garlanded house, and everywhere was heard her laughter. She patted the bridegroom on arm and cheek, and cried out, to guest after guest, that for two cents she would marry him herself. When the time came to throw rice after the departing couple, she was positively devil-may-care. Indeed, so extravagant was her pitching that one hard-packed handful of the sharp little grains hit the bride squarely in the face.

But when the car was driven off, she stood still looking after it, and there came from her downturned mouth a laugh not at all like her usual trill. 'Well,' she said, 'we'll see.' Then she was Mrs Ewing again, running and chirping and urging more punch on her guests.

Lolita wrote to her mother every week without fail, telling of her apartment and the buying and placing of furniture and the always new adventure of shopping; each letter concluded with the information that John hoped Mrs Ewing was well and sent her his love. The friends eagerly inquired about the bride, wanting to know above all if she was happy. Mrs Ewing replied that well, yes, she said she was. 'That's what I tell her every time I write to her,' she said. 'I say, "That's right, honey, you go ahead and be happy just as long as you can."'

It cannot be said in full truth that Lolita was missed in the town; but there was something lacking in the Ewing house, something lacking in Mrs Ewing herself. Her friends could not actually define what it was, for she went on as always, flirting the skirts of her little dresses and trying on her little hair ribbons, and there was no slowing of her movements. Still, the glister was not quite so golden. The dinners and the bridge games continued, but somehow they were not as they had been.

Yet the friends must realize she had taken a stunning blow, for Mardy left her; left her, if you please, for the preposterous project of getting married; Mardy, after all the years and all Mrs Ewing's goodness to her. The friends shook their heads, but Mrs Ewing, after the first shock, could be gay about it. 'I declare,' she said, and her laugh spiralled out, 'everybody around me goes off and gets married. I'm just a regular little old Mrs Cupid.' In the long line of new maids there were no Mardys; the once cheerful little dinners were gloomy with grease.

Mrs Ewing made several journeys to see her daughter and son-in-law, bearing gifts of black-eyed peas and tins of herring roe, for New Yorkers do not know how to live and such delicacies are not easily obtained up North. Her visits were widely spaced; there was a stretch of nearly a year between two of them, while Lolita and John Marble travelled in Europe and then went to Mexico. ('Like hens on hot griddles,' Mrs Ewing said. 'People ought to stay put.')

Each time she came back from New York, her friends gathered about her, clamoring for reports. Naturally, they quivered for news of oncoming babies. There was none to tell them. There was never any issue of those golden loins and that plank of a body. 'Oh, it's just as well,' Mrs Ewing said comfortably, and left the subject there.

John Marble and Lolita were just the same, the friends were told.

John Marble was as devastating as he had been when he first came to the town, and Lolita still had not a word to say for herself. Though her tenth wedding anniversary was coming close, she could not yet give shape to her dresses. She had closets of expensive clothes – when Mrs Ewing quoted the prices of some of the garments, the friends sucked in their breath sharply – but when she put on a new dress it might as well have been the old one. They had friends, and they entertained quite nicely, and they sometimes went out. Well, yes, they did seem so; they really did seem happy.

'It's just like I tell Lolita,' Mrs Ewing said. 'Just like I always say to her when I write: "You go ahead and be happy as long as you can." Because – Well, you know. A man like John Marble married to a girl like Lolita! But she knows she can always come here. This house is her home. She can always come back to her mother.'

For Mrs Ewing was not a woman who easily abandoned hope.

RYŪNOSUKE AKUTAGAWA *Hell Screen*

KINGSLEY AMIS *Dear Illusion*

SAUL BELLOW *Him With His Foot in His Mouth*

DONALD BARTHELME *Some of Us Had Been Threatening Our Friend Colby*

SAMUEL BECKETT *The Expelled*

JORGE LUIS BORGES *The Widow Ching – Pirate*

PAUL BOWLES *The Delicate Prey*

ITALO CALVINO *The Queen's Necklace*

ALBERT CAMUS *The Adulterous Woman*

TRUMAN CAPOTE *Children on Their Birthdays*

ANGELA CARTER *Bluebeard*

RAYMOND CHANDLER *Killer in the Rain*

EILEEN CHANG *Red Rose, White Rose*

G. K. CHESTERTON *The Strange Crime of John Boulnois*

JOSEPH CONRAD *Youth*

ROBERT COOVER *Romance of the Thin Man and the Fat Lady*

ISAK DINESEN *Babette's Feast*

MARGARET DRABBLE *The Gifts of War*

HANS FALLADA *Short Treatise on the Joys of Morphinism*

F. SCOTT FITZGERALD *Babylon Revisited*

IAN FLEMING *The Living Daylights*

E. M. FORSTER *The Machine Stops*

SHIRLEY JACKSON *The Tooth*

HENRY JAMES *The Beast in the Jungle*

M. R. JAMES *Canon Alberic's Scrap-Book*

JAMES JOYCE *Two Gallants*

FRANZ KAFKA *In the Penal Colony*

RUDYARD KIPLING *'They'*

D. H. LAWRENCE *Odour of Chrysanthemums*

PRIMO LEVI *The Magic Paint*

H. P. LOVECRAFT *The Colour Out Of Space*

MALCOLM LOWRY *Lunar Caustic*

CARSON MCCULLERS *Wunderkind*

KATHERINE MANSFIELD *Bliss*

ROBERT MUSIL *Flypaper*

VLADIMIR NABOKOV *Terra Incognita*

R. K. NARAYAN *A Breath of Lucifer*

FRANK O'CONNOR *The Cornet-Player Who Betrayed Ireland*

DOROTHY PARKER *The Sexes*

LUDMILLA PETRUSHEVSKAYA *Through the Wall*

JEAN RHYS *La Grosse Fifi*

SAKI *Filboid Studge, the Story of a Mouse That Helped*

ISAAC BASHEVIS SINGER *The Last Demon*

WILLIAM TREVOR *The Mark-2 Wife*

JOHN UPDIKE *Rich in Russia*

H. G. WELLS *The Door in the Wall*

EUDORA WELTY *Moon Lake*

P. G. WODEHOUSE *The Crime Wave at Blandings*

VIRGINIA WOOLF *The Lady in the Looking-Glass*

STEFAN ZWEIG *Chess*

a little history

Penguin Modern Classics were launched in 1961, and have been shaping the reading habits of generations ever since.

The list began with distinctive grey spines and evocative pictorial covers – a look that, after various incarnations, continues to influence their current design – and with books that are still considered landmark classics today.

Penguin Modern Classics have caused scandal and political change, inspired great films and broken down barriers, whether social, sexual or the boundaries of language itself. They remain the most provocative, groundbreaking, exciting and revolutionary works of the last 100 years (or so).

In 2011, on the fiftieth anniversary of the Modern Classics, we're publishing fifty Mini Modern Classics: the very best short fiction by writers ranging from Beckett to Conrad, Nabokov to Saki, Updike to Wodehouse. Though they don't take long to read, they'll stay with you long after you turn the final page.